Her Halloween Hunk

A SMALL TOWN HOLIDAY SWEET ROMANCE

SWEPT AWAY IN BUTTERCUP BAY
BOOK TWO

MOLLY ARDEN

Molly Arden
SWEET SMALL TOWN ROMANCE

Contents

CHAPTER 1

Greg

THE MORNING SUN is just beginning to rise over Buttercup Bay, casting a soft golden light across the town as I unlock the door to Buttercup Bakes. There's a familiar rhythm to these early hours—a comforting routine that's become second nature to me over the years. The scent of yeasty dough fills the air as I flip on the lights, illuminating the rustic charm of the place. Wooden beams stretch across the ceiling, their worn edges telling stories of the countless mornings they've seen. The vintage cash register sits proudly on the counter, a reminder of the bakery's history, and of the generations that came before me.

It's quiet now, the town still waking up as I go about my tasks—preparing the dough, measuring flour, and setting up the display cases for the day ahead. There's something peaceful about this time of day, before the hustle and bustle begins, when it's just me and the promise of what's to come.

I've always loved this town. Buttercup Bay has a way of wrapping itself around you, of making you feel like you belong, no matter who you are or where you come from. The people here are as much a part of this place as the cobblestone streets and the old oak trees that line them. They're good people—kind, dependable, and fiercely loyal to their own. It's a town where everyone knows your name, where neighbors look out for each other, and where there's a sense of continuity that's both comforting and rare.

The bell above the door jingles softly, and I glance up to see Mrs. Whittaker stepping inside, her usual briskness tempered by a warm smile. She's been coming to the bakery for as long as I can remember, always the first customer of the day.

"Morning, Greg," she says, her voice full of the no-nonsense cheer that's become her trademark. "Got any of those apple turnovers ready yet?"

"Just about," I reply, returning her smile as I pull a tray from the oven. The scent of cinnamon and baked apples fills the air, and I see her eyes light up. "Still warm."

She nods approvingly, tapping her fingers on the counter as I box up her order. "Best way to start the day, if you ask me. You've got a real gift, Greg."

"Thanks, Mrs. Whittaker," I say, handing her the box. "You've been saying that for years."

"And I'll keep saying it," she replies with a wink, digging into her purse for some cash. "This town wouldn't be the same without you, you know."

Her words bring a smile to my face, but there's a flicker of something else there, too—a quiet, unspoken longing that I can't quite shake. "I appreciate that," I say, sliding her change across the counter. "Have a good day."

She waves as she heads for the door, and I watch her go, the bell jingling softly in her wake. The bakery feels a little emptier without her in it, and I find myself lost in thought as I wipe down the counter, my mind drifting to the life I've built here.

It's a good life, by all accounts. The bakery is thriving, the town is full of people I care about, and I've got a place in the community that I'm proud of. But even with all that, there's a part of me that feels like something's missing. I've been in Buttercup Bay for years now, running the bakery, and building a life for myself. But as much as I love this town, there are moments when I can't help but wonder if there's more out there—if there's someone out there who's meant to share this life with me.

I shake off the thought, focusing on the task at hand. There's dough to be kneaded, bread to be baked, and a steady stream of customers who will soon be filing through the door. But even as I work, that quiet longing lingers in the back of my mind, a gentle reminder that while my life here is full, it's not quite complete.

The morning passes in a blur of activity—regulars stopping by for their usual orders, friendly faces exchanging pleasantries, and the hum of conversation filling the air. It's all familiar, all comforting in its own way. But as the hours tick by, I can't help but feel a twinge of restlessness, as if I'm waiting for something to change, for something—or someone—to walk through that door and turn my world upside down.

By the time the afternoon rolls around, the bakery has settled into a quiet lull, the rush of the morning giving way to the slower pace of the day. I find myself standing at the window, looking out at the town, my fingers absentmindedly tracing patterns on the cool glass. Buttercup Bay is beautiful this time of year, with trees dressed in shades of orange and red, their leaves dancing on the gentle breeze. The air is crisp and filled with the scent of autumn, a heady mix of fallen leaves, wood smoke, and the faintest hint of sea salt carried in from the bay.

The quaint storefronts lining Main Street are adorned with pumpkins and wreaths, their windows reflecting the warm glow of early Halloween decorations. A few locals stroll along the sidewalks, bundled up in cozy sweaters and scarves, their breath visible in small puffs as they chat and window-shop. It's a scene straight out of a postcard, picturesque and inviting, yet I can't shake the feeling that something's missing from this perfect tableau.

But still, moments like this remind me why I love this place so much—why I've stayed, even when I thought about leaving. There's a peace here, a sense of belonging that I've never found anywhere else. And yet, there's also that quiet ache in my chest, the one that whispers of dreams unfulfilled, of a heart that's still searching for its missing piece.

As the day draws to a close, I begin the familiar routine of closing up the bakery—wiping down the counters, sweeping the floors, locking the doors. The quiet of the empty shop settles around me, and I take a moment to stand in the middle of the room, letting the stillness wash over me. This is my place, my home, and I'm proud of what I've built here. But as I turn off the lights and step outside into the cool evening air, I can't help but feel that there's something waiting just around the corner for me. There has to be. This can't be all there is to life, right?

CHAPTER 2

Sophie

THE CAR RUMBLES over the narrow bridge, and I feel a strange mix of excitement and trepidation as I catch my first glimpse of Buttercup Bay. The town is every bit as picturesque as my friend Emilia promised—the kind of place that seems plucked from a postcard. The air is crisp, carrying the scent of cinnamon and apples, and as I drive down Main Street, I can't help but notice the pumpkins adorning nearly every doorstep. It's the perfect image of small-town charm.

But as I park my car and step out onto the cobblestone sidewalk, that initial excitement gives way to uncertainty. What am I doing here? A year ago, I was living in the fast lane—late-night meetings, endless projects, and the thrill of the city keeping me on my toes. Now, I'm standing in the middle of a town that feels like it's been frozen in time, with no clue if this is where I'm meant to be.

Emilia was convinced this was exactly what I needed—a personal retreat to clear my head and figure out what I wanted next. She told me that the slower pace and the sense of community in a place like Buttercup Bay would do me good. But as I take in the quaint shops and the slow-moving locals, I'm not so sure.

I glance around, feeling a bit like a fish out of water. The town is charming, there's no denying that, but can I really find clarity here? Or am I just running away from the life I left behind?

Pushing those thoughts aside, I decide to explore a bit. Maybe a walk will help ease this nagging doubt. I spot a bakery down the street, its large windows revealing a cozy interior that beckons to me. Buttercup Bakes. The name alone is inviting, and the idea of a warm coffee and something sweet is enough to draw me in.

As I step inside, I'm immediately greeted by the rich, comforting scent of fresh pastries and coffee. The space is exactly what you'd expect from a small-town bakery—rustic wooden tables, a chalkboard menu with today's specials scrawled in neat handwriting, and a display case filled with tempting treats. It's charming in the way that makes you want to linger.

Behind the counter, a man is busy arranging a tray of freshly baked muffins, their tops golden-brown and glistening. He's tall, with broad shoulders and strong, capable hands that move with practiced ease. There's something about his calm, steady presence that contrasts sharply with the rush of city life I'm used to—an unhurried air that seems to permeate the entire bakery. His movements are deliberate and focused, and each muffin is placed with care. When he looks up and spots me lingering near the entrance, he offers a warm smile that reaches his eyes. His welcoming demeanor immediately puts me at ease, making me feel less like a stranger and more like a regular customer, despite this being my first visit.

"Morning," he says, his voice smooth and welcoming. "What can I get for you?"

I return the smile, feeling a little of my earlier tension ease. "Just a coffee, please. And maybe one of those muffins?"

"Coming right up," he replies, moving with an easy grace as he pours the coffee. The rich aroma intensifies as the dark liquid streams into the cup. "You're new around here, aren't you?" he asks, his tone friendly and curious. His eyes flick up to meet mine, a hint of amusement playing at the corners of his mouth, as if he's privy to some local secret I've yet to discover.

"Is it that obvious?" I ask, trying to keep my tone light.

He chuckles, a sound that's both soft and genuine. "Well, Buttercup Bay's a small town. We tend to notice when someone new comes through."

I nod, taking in the details of the bakery as he works. "I'm just visiting, actually. A little retreat, I guess you could say."

"Good choice," he says, handing me the coffee and muffin. "This town's got a way of growing on you."

I sip the coffee, savoring the warmth that spreads through me. The rich aroma fills my senses, hinting at notes of caramel and vanilla. "I hope so," I reply, feeling the tension in my shoulders ease. "I could use a change of pace. The city can be... overwhelming sometimes."

He leans on the counter, his gaze steady but not probing. "If you're looking for a place to slow down, you've come to the right spot. Buttercup Bay's got its own rhythm."

There's something about his words that strikes a chord deep within me. Maybe it's the simplicity of them, the unadorned truth in his statement, or perhaps it's the idea that a slower rhythm could be exactly what I need to recalibrate my life. I'm not entirely sure yet, but as I take another sip of the rich, comforting coffee, I find myself wanting to believe it. The warmth of the mug seeps into my hands, and I can feel a small spark of hope igniting in my chest. Could this quaint town really be the fresh start I've been searching for? The thought is both exciting and terrifying, but for now, I allow myself to savor this moment of possibility.

"Thanks," I say, meaning it more than I expected. "I think I'll take my time figuring it out."

He smiles again, this time a little softer. "No rush. We're not going anywhere."

"My name's Sophie, by the way," I add, even though he didn't ask.

"I'm Greg," he replies with a warm smile. "I hope I'll see you around, Sophie."

I finish my coffee and muffin, the conversation lingering in my mind as I step back out into the crisp autumn air. The bakery was just one small stop, but something about it—about him—made me feel a bit more connected to this place. It's a small start, but it's something.

As I walk down Main Street, my steps are a little lighter. The uncertainty is still there, but it's not as overwhelming as before. Maybe Buttercup Bay is exactly what I need.

And as I continue exploring, I can't help but wonder if that man in the bakery was right. Maybe this town will grow on me. Maybe I'll find what I'm looking for here, in the most unexpected of places.

For now, though, I'm content to simply take it all in —one step at a time.

CHAPTER 3

Greg

I'VE SEEN all kinds of people walk through the doors of Buttercup Bakes—locals who've been coming in for years, their faces as familiar as the worn floorboards; tourists passing through, cameras dangling from their necks and maps clutched in their hands; even the occasional lost hiker looking for directions, their boots caked with mud and leaves. But Sophie was different.

From the moment she stepped inside, she stood out, not just because she was new in town. There was something about her—a kind of polish you don't see much around here. The way she moved, the way she held herself—it was clear she wasn't from a place like Buttercup Bay. But it wasn't just that. It was the way she looked around the bakery like she was taking it all in, trying to find her footing in a place that probably felt a million miles away from wherever she came from.

I'm wiping down the counter, replaying our brief conversation in my head. She'd ordered a coffee and a muffin—nothing special—but the way she spoke, her voice calm and measured, like she was used to making decisions quickly, efficiently… It was intriguing. Most people around here take their time, lingering over decisions, and chatting about the weather or what's going on in town. Sophie, though, seemed like someone who was used to things moving at a different pace.

I'm not sure why, but I find myself wondering what brought her here. Buttercup Bay isn't exactly a tourist hotspot, especially not in the fall. It's the kind of place people come to when they're looking for something specific—a working vacation, maybe, or just a break from the noise of wherever they're from.

She mentioned she was just visiting, something about a retreat. I couldn't help but notice the way she said it, almost like she was testing the word out, seeing how it felt on her tongue. A retreat. From what? From where?

The way her eyes darted away for a moment, the slight hesitation in her voice—it all hinted at something more. Was she running from something? Or maybe towards something? In Buttercup Bay, we were used to people seeking solace, but Sophie seemed different somehow. Her presence here felt charged with an energy that was hard to pin down, like she was a puzzle piece that didn't quite fit into our sleepy coastal town. I found myself oddly intrigued, wanting to know more about this mysterious woman and the story she wasn't telling.

It's funny, really. In a town as small and close-knit as Buttercup Bay, it's easy to fall into the comfortable illusion that you know everyone's story inside and out. You get used to the familiar faces at the local diner, the usual conversations at the post office, and the predictable rhythms of small-town life. But with Sophie, there's an intriguing mystery, a story I don't know yet—a rare blank page in our town's well-worn book of tales. And that's not something I come across very often in this place where gossip travels faster than the sea breeze. Her presence is like a pebble tossed into our still pond, causing ripples of curiosity that spread through our community. It's both unsettling and exciting, a reminder that even in a place as familiar as

Buttercup Bay, there's always room for the unexpected.

The bell above the door jingles as another customer walks in, but my thoughts keep drifting back to Sophie. There was something in her eyes—uncertainty, maybe, or curiosity. Whatever it was, it left an impression. And now, as I go about my day, I can't shake the feeling that I'd like to know more.

I finish with the last of the customers, the afternoon sun casting long shadows across the bakery floor, its golden light glinting off the glass display cases. The town is quieting down for the evening, the distant sound of seagulls and lapping waves replacing the usual bustle of daytime activity. I start the usual routine of closing up shop, my movements practiced and automatic after years of repetition. But even as I go through the motions—cleaning the tables with circular swipes, wiping down the counter until it gleams, flipping the sign to "Closed" with a satisfying click—my mind keeps returning to her.

Sophie's face floats in my thoughts, her enigmatic smile and those eyes that seemed to hold so many unspoken stories. I find myself wondering what brought her to our little coastal town and how long she plans to stay. As I sweep the floor, gathering the day's crumbs, I can't help but hope I'll see her again soon.

What is it about her that's got me so curious? Maybe it's the way she seemed a little out of place but not uncomfortable. Like she was looking for something, but she wasn't quite sure what it was yet. I wonder if she found any answers today, or if she'll be back tomorrow, still searching.

As I lock up and step outside, the cool evening air greets me, carrying the scent of fallen leaves and distant wood smoke. The town is peaceful at this hour, the kind of quiet that's easy to take for granted until you realize how rare it is. I lean against the door for a moment, looking down the street, imagining what it must look like to someone seeing it for the first time.

I can't help but hope that Sophie will come back. Not just because I'm curious, though I am, but because there's something about her that feels... unfinished. Like there's more to her story, more that I'd like to know. And maybe—just maybe—there's more to mine, too, if she decides to stick around.

With that thought lingering in my mind, I push off the door and start walking home. The day's over, but I can't help feeling like something new is just beginning. Maybe it's nothing. Or maybe, like the town itself, Sophie will grow on me in ways I can't quite predict yet.

Either way, I find myself looking forward to tomorrow a little more than usual.

CHAPTER 4

Sophie

THE BUTTERCUP INN is just as charming as the rest of the town—quaint, cozy, and utterly unlike anything I'm used to. The lobby is filled with comfortable armchairs, a crackling fireplace, and shelves lined with books that look like they've been read a hundred times. A large picture window lets in the late afternoon light, casting a warm, golden glow across the room.

As I check in, the innkeeper, Lily Thompson, greets me with a smile that crinkles the corners of her eyes. "Welcome to Buttercup Bay," she says, handing me a brass key. "Room 3, just up the stairs and to your right. Breakfast is at eight, and if you need anything, just let me know."

"Thank you," I reply, trying to match her warmth, but it feels a bit forced. My smile doesn't quite reach my eyes, and I can't shake the doubts that have been swirling in my mind since I arrived. This town is beautiful, no question, with its quaint charm and picturesque scenery, but can it really help me find the clarity I'm seeking? Or am I just fooling myself, thinking I can figure out my life in a place that feels so far removed from the one I know? The weight of my decision to come here suddenly feels heavy on my shoulders, and I wonder if I've made a mistake. Still, as I grip the brass key in my hand, I can't help but feel a tiny spark of hope that maybe, just maybe, Buttercup Bay holds the answers I've been searching for.

I hoist my heavy suitcase up the narrow, creaky wooden stairs, each step groaning under our combined weight. The sound reverberates through the otherwise hushed inn, making me feel self-conscious about disturbing the tranquil atmosphere. When I finally reach my room, I'm slightly out of breath but relieved to have arrived.

The space that greets me is small but undeniably cozy, with warm, honey-colored walls and a sturdy oak dresser tucked in the corner. A cheerful floral quilt adorns the bed, its soft blues and pinks a stark contrast to the minimalist grays I'm used to. The window, though a bit drafty, offers a charming view of the town square below, where a few locals stroll leisurely past quaint storefronts.

It's precisely the kind of place that should make me feel at ease, wrapped in small-town comfort and nostalgia. But as I set my suitcase down on the braided rug, all I can focus on is how jarringly different it is from the sleek, modern apartment I left behind in the city. The absence of stainless steel appliances and smart home devices is palpable, and I find myself wondering how long it will take to adjust to this simpler way of life.

I sit on the edge of the bed, taking in the silence. In the city, there was always noise—traffic, people, the constant hum of life moving at a breakneck pace. Here, it's quiet. Too quiet, maybe. I've never had this much space to just…think. And now that I do, I'm not sure what to do with it.

My thoughts drift back to the bakery. There was something about it—the warmth, the smell of freshly baked bread, the way it felt like a small oasis in the middle of this unfamiliar town. And then there was Greg. He was friendly and welcoming, but not in the overly familiar way that sometimes feels intrusive. His smile had been genuine, his eyes kind. I find myself thinking about that brief conversation more than I expected.

Maybe I'll go back. It could be nice to have a regular spot while I'm here, a place where I can feel a little more grounded. I make a mental note to visit again, perhaps tomorrow morning. The thought of establishing a routine, even a small one like getting my morning coffee from the same place, brings a sense of comfort. It's a tiny step towards making this unfamiliar town feel a bit more like home, at least for now.

Plus, the prospect of seeing Greg's friendly face again and maybe learning more about the local community is oddly appealing. I find myself looking forward to it, a small bright spot in the uncertainty of my current situation.

A soft knock on the door interrupts my thoughts. I open it to find Lily standing there, holding a small flyer.

"I thought you might be interested in this," she says, handing it to me. "We're having our annual Halloween Bash next week. We make lanterns, there's a Pumpkin Pie Contest, and this year, we're having a storytelling contest. It's a big event around here—lots of fun and a great way to meet people."

"Thank you," I say, taking the flyer. "I'll think about it."

She smiles again, giving me a knowing look. "It's a wonderful way to feel connected to the community. We'd love to have you join in."

After she leaves, I sit back down on the bed and look at the flyer. The event sounds fun, and maybe something I can get involved with. I'm involved with a lot of stuff back home, but none of the highlights sound like anything I'm good at. The closest would be the Pumpkin Pie contest, which sounds simple enough—bake a pumpkin pie, bring it to the town square, and see how it measures up against the others. But as I stare at the cheerful orange print, I realize it represents something more. It's an invitation to be a part of this town and to engage with the people who call Buttercup Bay home.

I glance out the window, watching as the sun begins to set, casting long shadows across the square. Maybe this is what I need—something small, something tangible to focus on. The idea of baking a pie is oddly comforting, a task with clear steps and a satisfying result. And maybe, just maybe, it's a way to start feeling like I belong here, even if it's just for a little while.

I decide then and there to enter the contest. It's a small step, but it feels like the right one—a tiny act of bravery in a sea of uncertainty. I'll bake a pie and take it to the square to join the other entries.

As I lie back on the bed, the doubts still linger, but they're softer now, less insistent. The city feels far away, and for the first time since I arrived, that thought doesn't make me uneasy. It makes me feel…lighter, somehow. Maybe I'm starting to see the appeal of this place—the slower pace, the sense of community. And maybe, just maybe, it's exactly what I need right now.

I close my eyes, letting the quiet of the inn wash over me. Tomorrow, I'll visit the bakery again, pick up the ingredients I need, and start preparing for the contest. Maybe the Buttercup Inn will let me use their oven.

This is such a small thing, but it feels like a step in the right direction. Maybe this town has more to offer me than I thought.

CHAPTER 5

Greg

THE BRASS BELL above the door jingles merrily, its familiar chime cutting through the cozy ambiance of the bakery. I glance up from my position behind the polished wooden counter, my hands pausing in their task of arranging a display of freshly baked croissants. My eyes widen slightly as I see Sophie walk into the shop, her presence immediately catching my attention.

It's only been a day since she was last here, her visit yesterday still fresh in my mind, but I find myself strangely pleased to see her again so soon. There's something about her that draws my attention, an indefinable quality that sets her apart from the usual flow of customers. Perhaps it's the way she carries herself, with a quiet confidence, or the spark of curiosity in her eyes as they sweep over the array of baked goods. Whatever it is, I can't help but feel a flutter of anticipation as she approaches the counter.

"Back so soon?" I ask, a smile tugging at the corners of my mouth.

She returns the smile, but there's a glint in her eye that's more focused, more determined. "I need some ingredients," she says, walking up to the counter. "I'm entering the Pumpkin Pie Contest."

That piques my interest. "The contest, huh? It's kind of a big deal around here. You sure you're ready for it?"

Her smile widens, and I can see the challenge in her expression. "I think I can handle it. I've got a few tricks up my sleeve."

"Is that so?" I lean on the counter, crossing my arms. "You know, I won last year's contest. It's not as easy as it looks."

She tilts her head slightly, considering me with a hint of amusement. Her eyes sparkle with a mix of challenge and mischief. "Well, I guess I'll just have to see if your winning streak ends this year," she says, her voice carrying a playful lilt. There's a confident set to her shoulders. "Maybe it's time for some fresh blood in the competition. Who knows? You might even pick up a new trick or two."

I chuckle, enjoying the playful banter. "Alright, let's see what you're working with. What ingredients do you need?"

As she rattles off her list—cinnamon, nutmeg, fresh pumpkin puree, and a few other essentials—I start gathering the items, moving efficiently around the kitchen. The familiar scents of autumn spices fill the air as I pull jars and containers from the shelves. But I can't resist giving her a bit of advice, my competitive spirit mingling with a genuine desire to see her succeed.

"You know," I say, placing a jar of ground cloves on the counter, "the secret to a really great pumpkin pie is in the balance. Too much of any one spice can overpower the others." I pause, considering whether to reveal one of my tricks. "And if you're feeling adventurous, a pinch of cardamom can add an unexpected depth of flavor."

She raises an eyebrow, clearly not convinced. "I

appreciate the tip, but I've got a method that works just fine."

"City style, huh?" I tease, placing the spices on the counter. "Precise measurements and all that?"

She nods, not missing a beat. "Exactly. Baking is a science, after all."

"Maybe," I say, leaning closer with a grin, "but it's also an art. Sometimes, you've got to trust your instincts."

She meets my gaze, her eyes locking with mine, and for a moment, the playful tone between us takes on a different, deeper edge. The bakery seems to fade away, leaving just the two of us in this charged instant. It's just a moment, fleeting yet intense, but it's enough to make me feel a flicker of something more—something that goes beyond friendly competition. A warmth spreads through my chest, and I find myself wondering if she feels it, too. The air between us crackles with unspoken possibilities, hinting at a connection that neither of us had anticipated when we first started discussing baking techniques.

But just as quickly, the moment passes, and she

smirks, breaking the tension. "We'll see which approach wins out at the contest."

"I guess we will," I reply, sliding the last of the ingredients across the counter. "But don't say I didn't warn you."

She laughs, a light, genuine sound that seems to fill the whole bakery. "You're on, Greg. May the best baker win."

As she gathers her items and heads for the door, I can't help but watch her go, my thoughts lingering on our conversation. There's a part of me that's intrigued by her confidence, by the way she's not afraid to challenge me. It's refreshing, really. Most people around here know my reputation as the go-to baker, and they don't often push back. But Sophie… she's different. And I like it.

I find myself thinking about her long after she's gone, the way her eyes sparkled with that playful challenge, the way she seemed so sure of herself. It's not just that she's entering the contest—it's the way she's approaching it, with that mix of precision and creativity that I can't quite pin down.

As I finish up for the day, I realize I'm looking forward to the contest more than I have in years.

Not just for the competition, but for the chance to see what Sophie's got up her sleeve. And maybe, just maybe, to see if there's more to this connection than just a newfound friendly rivalry.

The thought lingers with me as I lock up the bakery and step out into the cool evening air. There's a certain energy buzzing around me, something new, something different, something electric. It's as if the very atmosphere has shifted, charged with possibility. As I walk down the quiet street, the streetlights flickering to life one by one, I can't help but wonder where this unexpected turn of events might lead. What surprises might tomorrow bring? What new challenges and opportunities await? The night sky above seems to hold countless secrets, and for once, I'm eager to unravel them all.

Whatever happens, I know one thing for sure: this year's contest is going to be interesting.

CHAPTER 6

Sophie

THE MORNING SUN filters through the windows of Buttercup Bakes, casting a warm glow over the polished wooden floors and rustic furniture. The bakery is quiet at this hour, with only a few early risers sipping coffee and nibbling on pastries at the corner tables. It's peaceful, a stark contrast to the bustling city mornings I'm used to. And yet, there's something comforting about the stillness here, something that makes me feel at ease as I step inside.

Greg is behind the counter, moving with a practiced ease as he arranges fresh loaves of bread on display. His presence fills the space with a steady, reassuring warmth, and I find myself smiling as I approach him.

"Good morning, Sophie," he says, glancing up and giving me that easy, genuine smile that makes everything brighter. "Back for more already?" His eyes twinkle with a mix of warmth and amusement, as if he's pleased to see me but not entirely surprised by my return.

I laugh softly, brushing a strand of hair behind my ear. "I couldn't stay away. Plus, I wanted to talk to you about the Pumpkin Pie Contest."

His eyes light up with interest as he sets down the bread and leans casually against the counter, his flour-dusted hands leaving faint imprints on the polished surface. "Oh? How's the preparation going?" he asks, his voice tinged with genuine curiosity. There's a hint of excitement in his expression, as if he's already imagining the delicious possibilities of the contest.

"That's the thing," I admit, feeling a little self-conscious. "I'm really excited about the contest, but I don't have anywhere to practice my baking. The inn's kitchen is small, and I don't want to make a mess of it. I was thinking about trying to find somewhere else, but I'm not sure where to start."

Greg nods, considering my words. There's a moment of silence as he looks at me, his expression thoughtful. Then, without missing a beat, he says, "Why don't you practice here? You can use the bakery's kitchen."

I blink, taken aback by his offer. "Are you sure? I wouldn't want to impose..."

He waves off my concern with a dismissive gesture. "It's no trouble at all. I've got plenty of space back there, and I'd be happy to help if you need it. Besides," he adds with a playful smile, "I'd love to see what you come up with."

My heart swells with gratitude, and I can't help the smile that spreads across my face. "Thank you, Greg. That's incredibly generous of you."

He shrugs, but there's a warmth in his eyes that tells me he's pleased to be able to help. "Like I said, it's no trouble. And who knows? Maybe I'll pick up a few tips from you."

I laugh, feeling a flush of warmth at his words. "I'm not sure I'm the one who should be giving tips, but I'll do my best."

Our eyes meet, and for a moment, the world outside the bakery seems to fade away, leaving just the two of us standing there, sharing a quiet connection that feels deeper than anything we've shared before. There's something about Greg that puts me at ease, something that makes me feel like I can be myself around him. It's a feeling I haven't had in a long time, and I'm not quite sure what to make of it.

"You know," he says after a moment, his tone softening, "I've been thinking about the contest, too. It's a big deal around here, and I can tell you're really passionate about it. I think you're going to do great, Sophie."

His words, so genuine and sincere, make my heart flutter in a way that catches me off guard. A warmth spreads through my chest, and I find myself smiling despite my nerves. "Thanks, Greg. That means a lot to me," I say softly, meeting his gaze. There's a gentleness in his eyes that I hadn't noticed before, and it makes me feel both comforted and slightly flustered. I take a deep breath, trying to steady the sudden rush of emotions coursing through me.

He smiles, and there's a warmth in his gaze that sends a pleasant shiver down my spine. "You've got this. And like I said, I'm here if you need anything."

The conversation shifts to lighter topics after that—banter about the best types of pumpkin to use, the ideal pie crust, and the merits of various spices—but the warmth between us lingers, wrapping around me like a cozy blanket. I find myself laughing more easily, relaxing into the rhythm of our conversation as if we've known each other for much longer than just a couple of days. Greg's eyes crinkle at the corners when he chuckles, and I catch myself admiring how his whole face lights up when he's passionate about something—like his adamant defense of nutmeg as the superior pumpkin pie spice.

As we chat, I absently fiddle with the hem of my dress, surprised at how comfortable I feel. The nervousness from earlier has melted away, replaced by a gentle buzz of contentment. Our words flow effortlessly, punctuated by shared laughter and playful debates. When Greg dramatically recounts a disastrous attempt at making a lattice crust, complete with exaggerated hand gestures, I can't help but giggle, feeling a connection spark between us that goes beyond mere colleague camaraderie.

By the time I leave the bakery, the promise of using Greg's bakery kitchen for my practice sessions tucked securely in my mind, I feel lighter, more excited about the contest than ever before. And as I step out into the crisp morning air, I can't help but think that this town—this bakery, and Greg—are becoming more important to me than I expected.

As I walk back to the inn, my thoughts drift back to the moment we shared in the bakery, the connection that seemed to hum between us like an unspoken promise. There's something about Greg that draws me in, something that makes me want to know him better and spend more time with him. And with the contest coming up, I'll have plenty of opportunities to do just that.

A smile tugs at my lips as I think about the days ahead—about the time I'll spend in the bakery, practicing my recipes, and getting to know Greg even more. There's a flutter of anticipation in my chest, a sense of excitement that I haven't felt in a long time.

And as I step through the door of the inn, the thought occurs to me that maybe this is the beginning of something special.

CHAPTER 7

Sophie

THE WARMTH of the oven wraps around me as I stand in the middle of Buttercup Bakes kitchen, rolling out dough on the floured countertop. The air is filled with the sweet scent of cinnamon and nutmeg, mingling with the rich aroma of coffee brewing nearby. There's something soothing about the steady rhythm of baking—measuring, mixing, kneading—that feels like a balm to my restless mind.

I glance over at Greg, who's focused on perfecting the crust of his own pie. His movements are confident, sure, like he's done this a thousand times before. It's clear he knows his way around a kitchen, and I can't help but admire the ease with which he works. There's a quiet satisfaction in his expression that makes me wonder if he ever feels uncertain like I do.

"Need any help with that?" he asks, glancing up and catching me watching him.

I smile, shaking my head. "I think I've got it. But I'll let you know if I hit a snag."

He grins, a playful glint in his eyes. "Don't be afraid to ask. I've got a few tricks up my sleeve."

"Is that so?" I raise an eyebrow, mimicking his earlier teasing tone. "I thought you said baking was all about trusting your instincts." I can't help but smirk as I throw his own words back at him. There's something oddly satisfying about this playful banter, a comfortable rhythm we've fallen into without even realizing it. I watch him closely, curious to see how he'll respond to my gentle challenge.

He laughs softly, the sound warm and inviting. "It is. But a little experience doesn't hurt either."

I return to my dough, kneading it with renewed focus, but I can't ignore the comfortable silence that's settled between us. It's a silence that doesn't feel awkward or forced—it just is, natural and easy, like we've been doing this for much longer than a few days. The rhythmic motion of my hands working the dough becomes almost meditative, allowing my thoughts to wander. It's surprising how quickly I've started to feel at home in this bakery, in this town.

As I work, my thoughts begin to drift. I imagine what it might be like to have a place like this of my own—a bakery where I could bring together the sophistication of the city with the warmth I've found here in Buttercup Bay. The idea is both exhilarating and terrifying. Could I really do it? Could I build something like this, something that feels so personal and meaningful?

I sprinkle flour on the counter, trying to picture it. The sleek countertops I'm used to, but with wooden beams overhead, a chalkboard menu on the wall, and cozy seating where people could linger over coffee and pastries. It's a blend of everything I love—the elegance of the city and the welcoming charm of this town. The more I think about it, the more real it starts to feel, like a possibility I hadn't considered before.

"Penny for your thoughts?" Greg's voice pulls me out of my reverie.

I blink, realizing I've been lost in my imagination. "Oh, just thinking about what my bakery might look like if I ever had one."

He looks intrigued. "What would it be like?"

I pause, trying to put the vivid image in my head into words. "I think... it would be a mix of what I'm used to in the city and what I've found here in this charming town. Something modern but warm and inviting, with sleek countertops and rustic wooden accents. A place where people could come to relax, have a good cup of coffee, and maybe stay awhile. I'd want it to have big windows to let in natural light and comfortable seating areas where friends could catch up, or someone could curl up with a book. And, of course, there'd be display cases filled with an array of pastries and cakes that change with the seasons."

Greg nods thoughtfully. "Sounds like it could be something special."

I feel a flicker of excitement, but it's tempered by the familiar tug of doubt. "Maybe. But it's just an idea right now."

"Every great thing starts as an idea," he says, his

tone encouraging. "And if you ever want to make it more than that, you know where to find me."

His words catch me off guard, and I look up at him, meeting his steady gaze. There's no pressure in his expression, just a quiet confidence that makes me believe, if only for a moment, that this dream could actually come true.

"Thanks, Greg," I say softly, meaning it more than I expected.

He just smiles, turning back to his work. And I find myself smiling, too, feeling a warmth that has nothing to do with the oven. It's not just the bakery that's beginning to feel like home—it's the people, the sense of community that's starting to wrap itself around me, making me feel like I belong here.

As we continue baking, the afternoon light filters through the windows, casting a golden glow over the room. The quiet moments we share, the gentle banter, the simple act of working together—it all feels right in a way I hadn't anticipated.

For the first time in a long while, the future doesn't seem so uncertain. Instead, it feels full of possibilities, full of the life I could build here, in this little town, with the people who are becoming more important to me each day. Emilia was right; Buttercup Bay was the perfect place for a personal retreat.

The thought sends a thrill through me, a mix of excitement and nervous anticipation. I can almost see it unfolding before me—mornings spent in the bakery, afternoons exploring the town's hidden corners, evenings shared with new friends. It's a vision that's both comforting and exhilarating, like stepping onto solid ground after being adrift for so long. This place, with its quaint charm and welcoming inhabitants, is slowly but surely weaving itself into the fabric of my life, becoming not just a temporary stop, but a potential home.

And as I roll out the final piece of dough, I realize that I'm not just baking a pie. I'm starting to bake a new life—one that's a little sweeter, a little simpler, and a lot more meaningful than I ever imagined.

Greg

WHEN SOPHIE first suggested joining the Pumpkin Pie contest, I laughed it off as absurd. It was meant to be a joke, a playful jab at our wildly different approaches to baking: she, the meticulous measurer, and I, the throw-it-all-in-and-hope-for-the-best type. But before I knew it, the whole town had found out that the newcomer was joining the competition—they'd been buzzing about it like bees around a particularly sweet flower. Gossip spread faster than wildfire in our little community, and now, here I am, flour dusting my cheeks, rolling out dough for what's inexplicably become the most talked-about event of the Halloween season. The pressure's on, and I can't help but wonder if I've bitten off more than I can chew in this culinary showdown.

As I knead the dough, I steal a glance at Sophie, who's busy chopping pecans with the same focused precision she brings to everything she does. There's something about the way she moves—deliberate, confident—that I can't help but admire. But it's more than that. There's a part of me that's started to hope, despite myself, that this bake-off is just the beginning of something more.

"Better watch out, Greg," she teases, her eyes flicking up to meet mine. "I've got a secret ingredient that's going to blow your pie out of the water."

I chuckle, trying to keep things light. "Oh yeah? I'll believe it when I taste it."

She grins, and for a moment, the playful banter feels like a dance—a way to stay close without getting too close. But underneath it all, there's a tension that I can't ignore, a feeling that this isn't just about who makes the better pie. It's about something deeper, something that scares me a little because I'm not sure where it's heading.

Her smile lingers, warm and inviting, and I find myself mirroring it without even thinking. The kitchen suddenly feels smaller, more intimate, as if the rest of the world has faded away. I can hear the soft clink of her knife against the cutting board and smell the rich aroma of butter and cinnamon in the air. It's intoxicating, this moment we're sharing, and I'm acutely aware of every breath, every subtle shift of her body as she works.

I want to say something clever to keep this verbal sparring match going, but the words catch in my throat. There's an electricity crackling between us, unspoken but undeniable. It's thrilling and terrifying all at once, like standing on the edge of a cliff, knowing that one step could change everything. I'm not ready to take that step, not yet, but I can't deny the pull I feel towards her, stronger with each passing second.

As we work side by side, the bakery feels different. The usual rhythm of the place is still here—the soft hum of the oven, the scent of cinnamon and nutmeg in the air—but there's an added layer of energy, something electric that passes between us in the smallest of moments—a shared laugh bubbles up between us, light and carefree, easing the tension for a moment. The brush of our hands as we reach for the same mixing bowl sends a jolt of electricity through my fingertips, and I can't help but wonder if she feels it, too. The way her eyes linger on mine just a little too long before she looks away, a hint of a blush coloring her cheeks, speaks volumes in the silence. It's a dance of stolen glances and almost-touches, each adding fuel to the smoldering connection between us.

Is this just a friendly competition to her, or is there more? The thought sends a thrill through me, but it's quickly followed by a familiar pang of fear. What if I'm getting ahead of myself? What if, after this contest, she packs up and leaves Buttercup Bay behind? And what if I'm left here, missing her more than I should?

"Penny for your thoughts?" Sophie's voice pulls me back, and I realize I've been quiet for too long.

"Just thinking about how this contest might be tougher than I expected," I say, trying to keep my tone casual.

She laughs, a sound that makes the whole room feel warmer. "Good. I'd hate for it to be too easy for you."

There's that spark again, that playful challenge that makes me want to keep her close and never let go. But even as we joke and tease, I can't shake the feeling that this is more than just a game. It's a test, not just of our baking skills, but of what's happening between us.

As we continue preparing for the contest, trying out new recipes and subtle changes to old ones, the moments of intimacy come in waves—small, quiet, and significant. I notice the way she laughs when I tell a joke, how her eyes crinkle at the corners, and how her smile lingers long after the laughter fades. I notice how she leans a little closer when she's concentrating, and her focus sharpens as she measures out ingredients with the precision of a scientist. And I notice how, when we're both lost in our work, there's a comfortable silence between us, one that feels as natural as breathing.

It's in these moments that I realize just how much I care for her. It's not just about the way she fits so easily into the rhythm of the bakery or how she's brought a new energy to the place. It's about how she makes me feel—alive, hopeful, and more than a little terrified.

Because if I'm honest with myself, I know I'm starting to fall for her. And that scares me more than anything. I've always been careful with my heart, keeping it close and safe, especially after the last time I let someone in. But with Sophie, it's different. She's different.

There's a warmth to her presence that melts through the walls I've built around myself. Her laughter fills the bakery with a kind of joy I'd forgotten existed. And when our eyes meet across the kitchen, I feel a spark of something I can't quite name—something that makes my breath catch and my hands tremble ever so slightly.

It's not just attraction, though that's certainly part of it. It's the way she sees the world, and the passion she brings to everything she does. She challenges me, and pushes me to be better, not just as a baker but as a person. And that terrifies me because I know that if I let her in completely, there's no going back. The thought of losing her, of feeling that pain again, is almost paralyzing. But the thought of never knowing what we could be? That's somehow even worse.

The thought of her leaving, of this being just a temporary stop on her way to something else, twists my gut. I try to push the fear away, focusing instead on the task at hand. But it's there, lurking in the back of my mind, even as we finish up the preparations and start cleaning the kitchen.

"Ready for tomorrow?" she asks, wiping her hands on a towel and looking at me with that same mix of challenge and warmth that's been driving me crazy all day.

"As ready as I'll ever be," I reply, forcing a smile.

But as we say our goodbyes and she leaves the bakery, the truth settles in my chest like a weight. I'm not just ready for tomorrow—I'm dreading it. Because no matter how the contest turns out, it feels like a turning point, a moment where everything could change.

And for the first time in a long time, I'm not sure if I'm ready for that.

CHAPTER 9

Sophie

BUTTERCUP BAY HAS NEVER LOOKED as magical as it does tonight.

The town square is transformed into a Halloween wonderland, with strings of orange and purple lights twinkling overhead and jack-o'-lanterns glowing on every corner. Their flickering faces cast dancing shadows across the cobblestone streets, creating an enchanting play of light and dark.

The scent of caramel apples and spiced cider fills the crisp evening air, mingling with the sound of laughter and the lively chatter of townspeople enjoying the festivities. Children in colorful costumes dart between adults, their excited squeals adding to the festive atmosphere. For the first time since I arrived, I feel a sense of belonging, like I'm part of something bigger than myself. The warmth of community envelops me, and I find myself smiling at strangers, caught up in the infectious joy of the celebration. It's as if the magic of Halloween has woven its spell over the entire town, bringing us all together in a shared moment of wonder and delight.

I weave through the crowd, smiling at familiar faces, and exchanging friendly nods and waves. It's strange to think how quickly this town has become a part of me, how its warmth and simplicity have started to seep into my bones. There's a comfort here that I hadn't expected, a feeling that maybe, just maybe, I could find my place in this little corner of the world.

As I approach the contest table, my heart does a little flip. Greg is already there, setting up his pie with a focused look on his face. He glances up as I arrive, and our eyes meet across the table. There's a tension in that glance, something unspoken but undeniable. I can feel it, like a current running between us, pulling us closer even as I try to keep my distance. The bustling fair around us seems to fade away, leaving just this moment suspended in time. His gaze holds mine for a beat longer than necessary, and I find myself holding my breath, caught in the magnetic pull of his presence. It's as if the air between us has become charged, crackling with possibility and unresolved emotions.

I force myself to look away, busying my hands with arranging my own pie, but I can still feel the weight of his eyes on me, a tangible reminder of the complicated feelings we're both trying to navigate.

"Ready for the big showdown?" I ask, trying to keep my tone light.

He grins, but there's a softness in his eyes that makes my breath catch. "As ready as I'll ever be. How about you?"

"Same," I reply, though my nerves are jangling. It's not just the competition—it's everything. The way the town has welcomed me, embracing me with open arms and warm smiles, the way Greg looks at me with those deep, understanding eyes that seem to see right through to my soul, the way I'm starting to feel like this place could be more than just a temporary stop—it could be home.

But home is such a loaded word, isn't it? A word heavy with expectations and memories, both good and bad. It's a word I've always associated with the bustling city streets, the familiar rhythm of subway trains, the life I painstakingly built there over years of hard work and determination. And yet, here I am, standing in a small-town square surrounded by quaint shops and friendly faces, feeling something I never thought I'd feel again—a sense of belonging, a warmth that spreads through my chest and settles deep in my bones. It's both exhilarating and terrifying, this unexpected connection to a place I barely know.

The contest begins, and the crowd gathers around to watch. As I serve slices of my pie, I can't help but steal glances at Greg. He's chatting with the townspeople, laughing, making everyone feel at ease. It's one of the things I admire about him—his ability to connect with people, to make them feel like they matter. It's something I've always struggled with, always keeping a bit of myself hidden, afraid to let anyone get too close.

The judging starts, and the tension between Greg and me is almost palpable. It's not just about whose pie is better—there's more at stake, something deeper that neither of us is quite ready to confront. As the judges deliberate, I find myself holding my breath, not just for the outcome but for what this moment represents.

And then, just as they're about to announce the winner, my phone buzzes in my pocket. I glance down at the screen, and the name flashing there sends a jolt of reality through me—Rebecca, my boss from the city. My heart pounds as I step away from the table, the noise of the crowd fading as I answer the call.

"Sophie, I'm glad I caught you," Rebecca's voice is brisk, businesslike. "We've been reviewing the applications for the new position, and I wanted to offer it to you. It's a significant promotion, with a substantial salary increase. We need an answer by the end of the week."

Her words hit me like a cold splash of water, jolting me back to a reality I'd almost forgotten. The city. My career. Everything I've worked for, everything I thought I wanted, right there within my grasp. And yet, as I stand here, with the sounds of the Halloween Bash and Buttercup Bay behind me—the laughter, the music, the gentle lapping of waves against the shore—the thought of going back doesn't bring the rush of excitement it once did.

Instead, it brings a wave of uncertainty, fear, and something else I can't quite name. My mind races, flashing through images of my life in the city—the endless meetings, the late nights at the office, the constant pressure to climb higher. Then, it shifts to the warmth and simplicity I've found here in this small coastal town. The contrast is stark, leaving me feeling dizzy and conflicted.

"I... I need some time to think about it," I say, my voice shaky.

"Of course," Rebecca replies, though I can sense the impatience in her tone. Her fingers drum a rapid staccato on her desk in the background. "But don't take too long. We need someone who's fully committed." She pauses. "The team's counting on you, and frankly, so am I. This opportunity won't wait forever, you know."

Committed. The word echoes in my mind as I hang up and slowly walk back to the bake-off table. The judges have just announced the winner—Greg—and he's being congratulated by everyone around him. But as I approach, he looks up, and something in my expression makes him pause.

"What's wrong?" he asks, his voice low, concerned.

I force a smile, trying to push down the turmoil swirling inside me. "Nothing, just... a call from back home. My boss offered me a promotion."

He's quiet for a moment, his eyes searching mine. "And what are you going to do?"

"I don't know," I whisper, the truth spilling out before I can stop it. "I thought I knew what I wanted when I came to Buttercup Bay, but now... I'm not so sure. I've had some time to think and…" I trail off, not quite knowing how to answer.

Greg's hand brushes mine, a brief touch that sends warmth through me. "You'll figure it out," he says softly. "Whatever you decide, it'll be the right choice for you."

But will it? I wonder, as I look around the town square, at the people who have welcomed me with open arms, at the life I've started to imagine here. Can I really walk away from all of this? From Greg? Or am I fooling myself, thinking I can belong in a place like this?

As the night continues, I find myself drifting through the festivities, my mind a whirl of confusion. The Halloween Bash is everything I could have wanted—a celebration of community, of connection. But the call from Rebecca has shaken me to my core, bringing all my fears and doubts rushing to the surface.

I thought I was starting to figure things out, that I was finding my place here in Buttercup Bay. But now, I'm not sure of anything. The life I've always known, the career I've worked so hard for—it's all within my reach. But is it really what I want anymore? Or is there something else, something deeper, that I've been searching for all along?

The string lights twinkle above me, casting a warm glow over the town square, but their cheerful radiance feels at odds with the turmoil in my heart. I watch couples sway to the music, friends laugh over shared jokes, and children dart between adults' legs, their costumes a blur of color and imagination. It's a scene of perfect small-town contentment, the very thing I came here for to get away from what I'd always known.

But Rebecca's voice echoes in my mind, reminding me of the world I left behind. The fast-paced city life, the thrill of chasing stories, the satisfaction of seeing my byline in print—it's all calling me back. Yet, as I stand here, surrounded by the warmth of Buttercup Bay, I can't help but wonder if I've stumbled upon something far more precious than professional success. Have I found a sense of belonging that I've been craving all along, without even realizing it?

As I watch the lanterns float up into the night sky, carried by the breeze, I realize that I'm standing at a crossroads. And no matter which path I choose, something will be left behind.

The question is, what am I willing to sacrifice? And can I live with the choice I'm about to make?

CHAPTER 10

Greg

THE ELECTRIC EXCITEMENT of the Halloween Bash still crackles in the crisp autumn air, but my mind is consumed by a single image: Sophie's face when she broke the news about her promotion. I can't shake the memory of the conflict swirling in her deep brown eyes; the hesitation etched in the furrow of her brow.

Now, as I wander through the hushed streets of Buttercup Bay, my footsteps echoing off the quaint storefronts and charming cottages, the same thoughts keep circling in my mind like relentless vultures—she's going to leave. The realization hits me with each step: she's going to leave this sleepy coastal town behind, chasing her dreams to the big city. And I'm going to be left here, rooted in place, wondering what might have been if I'd only found the courage to speak up, to fight for us. The weight of unspoken words and missed opportunities settles heavily on my shoulders as I trudge on, the gentle lapping of the bay a melancholy soundtrack to my spiraling thoughts.

I've always prided myself on being content with my life here. The bakery, the town, the people—I belong here. But with Sophie, it's different. She's brought something new into my world, something I didn't even know I was missing. And now, just when I'm starting to realize how much she means to me, she might be slipping away.

I keep replaying our conversation in my head, trying to convince myself that I'm overreacting. But the truth is, I've seen this before. People come and go in Buttercup Bay. They visit, and they fall in love with the charm of the place, but when it comes down to it, they go back to their real lives. Lives that don't include small-town bakers like me.

It's a pattern I've witnessed time and time again: a bittersweet cycle of arrivals and departures. The tourists come, enchanted by our quaint streets and friendly faces, but eventually, the allure of their bustling cities and promising careers beckons them home. And I'm left behind, a fixture in this picturesque postcard town, wondering if I'll ever be more than just a fleeting memory in someone's summer romance.

The thought gnaws at me as I step into the bakery, the familiar scent of flour and sugar doing little to calm my nerves. I go through the motions of closing up for the night, but my mind is elsewhere, stuck on the image of Sophie walking out of my life, taking with her the possibility of something more.

What did I expect? That she'd give up her career, her life in the city, for a small-town guy who spends his days kneading dough? I've always known who I am, and what I have to offer, and it's never been much. But with Sophie, it feels like even less.

The bell above the door jingles, pulling me out of my thoughts. I look up to see my sister, Emma, standing there, a concerned look on her face.

"Hey," she says softly, stepping inside. "I saw you walking back from the square. You looked… troubled."

I force a smile, but it doesn't reach my eyes. "Just a lot on my mind."

Emma gives me that knowing look, the one she's perfected after years of being the town's unofficial therapist. "It's about that new girl I've seen you hanging out with, isn't it?"

I don't say anything, but I know she can see the answer in my expression. "Her boss called tonight. Offered her a promotion or something."

"She's got a big decision to make," Emma continues, her voice gentle. "But so do you, Greg."

I frown, not understanding. "What do you mean?"

Emma steps closer, placing a hand on my arm. "You're part of this community. You belong here, and everyone knows it. But you've got to decide if you're going to fight for what you want or if you're going to let fear hold you back."

Her words hit me hard, cutting through the fog of doubt clouding my mind. "I don't know if I'm enough to make her stay, Em. She's got so much waiting for her back in the city."

Emma squeezes my arm, her eyes kind but firm. "Greg, you don't have to be anything more than who you are. You've built a life here, one that's full of love and warmth. Maybe Sophie just needs to see that she can be a part of it, too." She pauses, her gaze softening as she searches my face. "Think about it. The community gatherings, the way everyone pitches in during harvest season, and the quiet evenings by the lake. These things make this place special, and you're at the heart of it all. Sophie's seen glimpses, but have you really shown her what it means to belong here?"

I want to believe her. I want to believe that what I have to offer is enough, that this town, this life, could be enough for Sophie. But the fear still lingers, gnawing at the edges of my resolve.

"What if she leaves anyway?" I ask, my voice barely above a whisper.

Emma smiles sadly. "Then you'll let her go, knowing you gave it your all. But don't let her leave without knowing how you feel. Don't let fear keep you from fighting for what you want."

I nod slowly, though the heavy knot in my stomach remains, twisting and churning with anxiety. My sister's right—I can't simply stand by and let Sophie slip away without putting up a fight. But the thought of truly opening up, of risking my heart again after so long, terrifies me to my core. The last time I let someone in and allowed myself to be vulnerable, it didn't end well. The pain of that experience still lingers, a dull ache that flares up whenever I consider getting close to someone new. I'm not sure I can go through that emotional upheaval again; I'm not sure I have the strength to piece myself back together if things fall apart. Yet, a small voice inside whispers that Sophie might be worth the risk.

As Emma leaves, I find myself alone in the bakery, the silence pressing in on me. This place has always been my refuge, my sanctuary. But tonight, it feels different—empty, almost, without Sophie's presence. I didn't realize how much I'd come to rely on the sound of her laughter, the way she lights up the room just by being in it.

I stand there for a long time, trying to sort through my tangled emotions. I've always been the steady one, the rock that people can depend on. But right now, I feel anything but steady. I feel like I'm standing on the edge of something, and I'm not sure if I have the courage to take the leap.

As I finally lock up and head home, the weight of my thoughts follows me. The town is quiet, the streets empty, but I can't shake the feeling that everything's about to change. And I'm not sure if I'm ready for it.

The stars are out, shining brightly in the clear night sky, their distant twinkle a stark contrast to the turmoil within me. I tilt my head back, searching for answers in the vast expanse above, but they do little to lift the heaviness in my chest. The cool night air brushes against my skin, carrying with it the faint scent of salt from the nearby ocean. I want to believe that Sophie could choose Buttercup Bay, that she could see the beauty in this small coastal town and the life we could build here together. That she could choose me, with all my flaws and imperfections. But the fear of being left behind, of being not enough to keep her here, is overwhelming. It creeps into my thoughts, wrapping around my heart like a vise, threatening to squeeze out any hope I dare to harbor.

I've always known where I belong, but now, with Sophie in the picture, I'm starting to question everything. And as much as I want to fight for her, I'm not sure if I have the strength to do it.

Because if she leaves, I'm not sure I'll ever be the same.

CHAPTER 11

Sophie

THE MORNING LIGHT filters through the delicate lace curtains of my cozy room at the Buttercup Inn, casting a soft, warm glow on the intricately quilted bedspread. I've been awake for hours, lying here motionless, staring at the ornate plaster ceiling, replaying Rebecca's words over and over in my mind like a broken record.

"A significant promotion with a substantial salary increase," she had said, her voice filled with excitement. It's everything I've worked tirelessly for, every late night and missed weekend, everything I thought I wanted when I first stepped into the corporate world. But now, with the weighty decision looming over me like a storm cloud, I feel nothing but a gnawing uncertainty that threatens to consume me. The gentle ticking of the antique clock on the nightstand seems to mock my indecision, each second bringing me closer to a choice I'm not sure I'm ready to make.

Buttercup Bay has a way of getting under your skin. It's not flashy or fast-paced; it's not the kind of place that would usually draw someone like me in. But there's something here, something I've been searching for without even realizing it—a sense of belonging, of community, of peace. And then there's Greg.

Greg. His name alone makes my heart squeeze, sending a flutter of warmth through my chest. It's as if the mere thought of him ignites a spark within me, one that threatens to burst into a roaring flame at any moment. His gentle smile, his kind eyes, the way he looks at me like I'm the only person in the world—it all comes rushing back in an instant, leaving me breathless and yearning for more.

I can still see the look in his eyes when I told him about the job offer—supportive, but with an undercurrent of something else. Disappointment? Fear? I don't know. I've been trying to figure it out, but the more I think about it, the more tangled my emotions become. His brows had furrowed slightly, creating a tiny crease between them that I longed to smooth away with my fingertip. His lips had curved into a smile, but it didn't quite reach his eyes, leaving me wondering what thoughts were swirling behind that carefully composed expression.

Every time I replay that moment in my mind, I catch another nuance, another flicker of emotion that I missed before. It's like trying to solve a puzzle with pieces that keep shifting and changing shape. One minute, I'm certain he was proud of me; the next, I'm convinced he was silently pleading with me to stay. The uncertainty gnaws at me, leaving me restless and second-guessing every interaction we've had since.

I need to clear my head, so I dress quickly and head downstairs, my footsteps echoing in the empty stairwell. The inn is unusually quiet this morning, the usual bustle subdued as if even the town itself is giving me space to think.

The floorboards creak softly beneath my feet as I make my way through the hallway, the scent of freshly brewed coffee guiding me forward. I find Lily in the dining room, her auburn hair catching the early morning light as she sits at a corner table, sipping coffee and reading the local paper. The rustle of pages and the soft clink of her mug against the table are the only sounds breaking the stillness.

"Morning," she says with a smile, folding the paper and setting it aside. "You look like you've got the weight of the world on your shoulders."

I sigh, sliding into the chair across from her. "It feels that way."

Lily pours me a cup of coffee and pushes it across the table. "Talk to me. What's going on?"

I take a sip, savoring the warmth before setting the mug down. "I got a job offer. A promotion, actually. It's everything I've been working toward."

Lily raises an eyebrow. "But?"

"But... I don't know if it's what I want anymore," I admit, the words tumbling out before I can stop them. "I've spent my whole life chasing success, climbing the ladder, and now that I'm so close, I'm not sure if that life still fits."

She nods thoughtfully, leaning back in her chair. "You know, Sophie, sometimes what we think we want isn't what we need. Buttercup Bay has a way of showing people what really matters."

I look at her, searching for answers. "What if I'm just scared? What if I'm making a mistake by walking away from everything I've worked for?"

Lily's eyes twinkle with that familiar mix of mischief and wisdom. "Mistakes are part of life, Sophie. But so is finding where you belong. And sometimes, you have to take a leap of faith to get there."

Her words resonate with me, but they don't make the decision any easier. "I feel like I'm being pulled in two directions. I've always been about the city, the hustle, the achievement. But here... it's different. It's slower, yes, but it's also fuller, and more connected. I'm starting to wonder if this is what I've been searching for all along."

Lily smiles warmly, her hand reaching across the worn wooden table to squeeze mine with surprising strength. "Only you can decide what's right for you, Sophie. But don't let fear make the decision for you. Sometimes, the path that scares us the most is the one we need to take." Her eyes, filled with decades of hard-earned wisdom, hold my gaze steadily. "Whatever you choose, make sure it's because your heart is pulling you there, not because you're running from something else."

I nod, feeling a little lighter, but still not entirely sure. "Thanks, Lily. I needed that."

"Anytime, darling," she says with a wink. "And remember, Buttercup Bay isn't going anywhere. But you've got to figure out where your heart wants to be."

As I leave the inn, Lily's words echo in my mind. Where does my heart want to be? The answer should be simple, but it's not. I find myself wandering through the town, letting the familiar sights and sounds wash over me. The smell of fresh bread from the bakery, the cheerful greetings from the shopkeepers, the warmth of the sun on my face —it all feels like home, more so than I ever imagined it could.

I end up at the small park near the town square, a tranquil oasis amidst the bustling town. The air is filled with the gentle cooing of pigeons and leaves rustling in the breeze. On a weathered wooden bench, Mrs. Whittaker, a longtime resident with silver hair and kind eyes, feeds the birds. She looks up as I approach, her sharp eyes taking me in with a knowing glance. There's a wisdom in her gaze that speaks of years spent observing the comings and goings of Buttercup Bay, and I can't help but feel she sees right through me.

"Morning, Sophie," she says, patting the bench beside her. "Come sit with me."

I sit down, feeling the weight of my thoughts pressing down on me like a heavy blanket. Mrs. Whittaker is one of those people who always seems to know what you're thinking, even before you do. Her piercing gaze makes me feel like an open book, pages fluttering in the breeze for her to read at will. I've seen her around a time or two during my stay here in Buttercup Bay, and we've chatted briefly about the weather and the local gossip, but nothing substantial. There's an air of mystery about her, as if she holds the secrets of the town close to her chest, waiting for the right moment to share them.

"You've got something on your mind," she says, not unkindly.

I nod, staring at the ground. "I got a job offer. A big one. It's what I've always wanted, but now... I'm not so sure."

Mrs. Whittaker nods as if she's heard this all before. "Let me ask you something, Sophie. What makes you happy? Not what you think should make you happy, but what actually does?"

I'm taken aback by the question. It's so simple, yet so profound. "I don't know," I say honestly. "I thought it was my career, the success, the fast-paced life. But now..." I trail off.

She pats my hand, her touch warm and comforting. "You're not the first person to come here thinking they knew what they wanted, only to find out that maybe they didn't. Buttercup Bay has a way of showing people what really matters."

I smile at the echo of Lily's words. "You sound like Lily."

Mrs. Whittaker chuckles. "Smart girl, that one. But she's right. You've got to think about what makes your heart sing, Sophie. Is it the city, the job, the hustle? Or is it the warmth of a small town, the connection to people, the possibility of something real with someone like Greg?"

Her words strike a chord deep within me, resonating through my very core. I close my eyes momentarily, letting the weight of her wisdom settle over me. I think about how Greg looks at me, his warm gaze filled with genuine affection and understanding. The way he makes me feel—safe, understood, valued—is unlike anything I've experienced. It's a feeling that wraps around me like a cozy blanket on a chilly evening.

I think about the bakery, with its inviting aroma of freshly baked bread and sweet pastries. The quaint town of Buttercup Bay, with its charming streets and friendly faces, has already begun to feel like home. The life I've started to imagine here is so different from what I had envisioned for myself, yet it feels right in a way I can't quite explain. It's not the life I meticulously planned out in my planner back in the city, with its rigid schedules and lofty career goals. But maybe, just maybe, it's the life I need—a life filled with warmth, connection, and the promise of something real and lasting.

As I walk back to the inn, Mrs. Whittaker's question keeps playing in my mind: What makes you happy? And as I let the question settle, I begin to realize that maybe I've been searching for the wrong things. Maybe happiness isn't about fitting into a mold or achieving a certain level of success. Maybe it's about finding where you feel at home, where you feel like you belong.

And right now, Buttercup Bay feels more like home than anywhere else ever has.

The decision isn't easy, but as I sit down at the small desk in my room and pick up the phone, I know what I have to do. My heart is here, in this town, with these people, with Greg. It's time to stop running and start building the life I truly want.

I dial Rebecca's number, my hand trembling slightly as I hold the phone to my ear. When she answers, I take a deep breath, feeling a sense of clarity I haven't felt in a long time.

"Rebecca," I say, my voice steady. "I appreciate the offer, but I've decided to stay in Buttercup Bay. It's where I belong."

As the words leave my mouth, I feel a weight lift off my shoulders. For the first time in a long while, I feel at peace with my decision. I'm choosing what makes me happy, what feels like home.

And as I hang up the phone, I know that the life I've always wanted isn't in the city—it's right here, in Buttercup Bay.

CHAPTER 12

Greg

I **ROLL** out dough on the countertop, but my heart isn't in it. My mind keeps drifting back to Sophie, to the way her face looked when she told me about the job offer. I can still see the uncertainty in her eyes, the way she seemed torn between two worlds. And now, the gnawing fear that she's going to choose the city over Buttercup Bay—over me—has taken root in my chest.

I try to shake it off, focusing on the task at hand, but it's no use. The idea of losing her has burrowed deep into my thoughts, making it impossible to concentrate. The doorbell chimes, and I glance up, expecting a customer, but my heart skips a beat when I see Sophie standing there, slightly out of breath, her eyes bright with resolve.

"Greg," she says, her voice trembling slightly as she steps inside. "I need to talk to you."

There's something in her tone, something that makes my heart race with both hope and fear. A mix of emotions flashes across her face, and I can't quite read what she's thinking. I wipe my hands on a towel, trying to steady myself and hide the slight tremor in my fingers. "What's going on, Sophie?" I ask, my voice coming out steadier than I feel. The air between us seems charged with anticipation, and I brace myself for whatever she's about to say.

She takes a deep breath, her gaze locking onto mine. "I've made a decision."

My stomach drops. I brace myself for the worst, for the words I've been dreading ever since she told me about the job offer. But as she steps closer, there's a new light in her eyes, a certainty that wasn't there before.

"I'm staying," she says, her voice strong and clear. "I turned down the job offer. Buttercup Bay is where I belong."

For a moment, I'm too stunned to speak. The relief that washes over me is so overwhelming that it leaves me breathless, my heart pounding in my chest. A thousand thoughts race through my mind, but I can't seem to form a single coherent sentence. "You're... staying?" I manage to say at last, my voice thick with emotion, barely above a whisper. I search her face, afraid I might have misheard, terrified that this might be some cruel dream I'm about to wake up from.

Sophie nods, her eyes shining with unshed tears. "Yes. I've been searching for a place where I feel like I belong, and I realized that it's right here. With you."

The words hit me like a tidal wave, washing away all the doubts and fears that have been haunting me for so long. I take a tentative step toward her, my legs suddenly unsteady, my heart pounding so hard I'm certain she must hear it. My voice trembles as I speak, hope and disbelief warring within me. "You're sure? This is what you want?" I search her eyes, desperate for confirmation, terrified that I might have misunderstood or that she might change her mind at any moment. The air between us feels charged, electric with possibility and the weight of this life-altering decision.

She closes the distance between us, reaching out to take my hands in hers. "I've never been more sure of anything in my life. I don't want to run anymore. I want to build a life here with you."

Her confession is like a lifeline, pulling me out of the darkness that's been weighing me down. I can feel the last remnants of my fear melting away, replaced by a joy so profound it almost brings me to my knees. I've spent so long worrying that I wasn't enough, that she'd leave and I'd be left behind. But now, hearing her say these words, I realize that I've been enough all along. And so has she.

"Sophie," I say, my voice trembling with emotion. "I've been so afraid that you'd leave, that I wasn't enough to make you stay. But hearing you say this... I can't even begin to tell you how much it means to me."

She smiles through her tears, squeezing my hands. "You are enough, Greg. You always have been. I was the one who needed to figure out where I belonged. And now I know."

The tension that's been hanging between us breaks, and before I know it, I'm pulling her into my arms, holding her close as if I'm afraid she might slip away. But she's here, solid and real, and when I look into her eyes, I see the same relief, the same joy, mirrored back at me.

"Sophie," I whisper, my voice thick with emotion. "I love you. I didn't want to say it before because I was afraid it would scare you away, but I can't hold it in any longer. I love you, and I want to build a life with you here, in Buttercup Bay."

Her eyes fill with tears, but she's smiling, a smile so full of love that it makes my heart swell. "I love you too, Greg. More than I ever thought possible."

And then, before I can say another word, she leans in, and our lips meet in a kiss that's everything I've been waiting for and more. It's filled with passion and relief, with all the emotions we've been holding back finally spilling over like a dam bursting.

Her arms wrap around my neck, her fingers tangling in my hair, and I pull her closer, my hands splaying across her back. I deepen the kiss, pouring everything I feel into this one perfect moment. The world around us fades away, and all I can focus on is the softness of her lips, the warmth of her body against mine, and the overwhelming sense that this is exactly where I'm meant to be. It's as if every moment in my life has been leading up to this, and now that it's here, I never want it to end.

When we finally pull back, we're both breathless, but the connection between us feels stronger than ever. I press my forehead to hers, feeling the steady beat of her heart against mine.

"We belong together," she whispers, and I know she's right. We don't have to change who we are to be loved and accepted. We belong, just as we are, here in Buttercup Bay with each other.

"We do," I agree, my voice soft but full of conviction. "And we'll face whatever comes next together."

As we stand in the warmth of the bakery, holding each other close, I feel a sense of peace settle over me. The future feels bright and full of promise, and for the first time in a long time, I'm not afraid. Because I know that no matter what happens, we'll face it together. We've found our place, our home, in each other.

And as I kiss her again, I know that this is just the beginning of our story—a story of love, belonging, and the life we'll build together in this little town that brought us both home.

CHAPTER 13

Sophie

THREE MONTHS LATER

THE SMELL of fresh paint and sawdust lingers in the air as I step into what will soon be my very own bakery—an add-on to Buttercup Bakes. This town has a way of surprising me, of giving me things I never knew I wanted, and standing here now, in the middle of this space that's slowly taking shape, I feel a sense of contentment that I've never felt before.

I run my fingers along the smooth, polished surface of the countertops—sleek and modern, a nod to the city life I've left behind, but softened by the rustic wooden beams that line the ceiling, adding warmth and character. The chalkboard menu on the wall still needs to be filled in, but I can already picture it —handwritten specials, the kind that change with the seasons, inviting customers to linger over a cup of coffee and a freshly baked pastry.

This place is me—a blend of where I've come from and where I am now, a perfect reflection of the journey I've taken to get here. The rustic wooden beams and sleek, modern countertops create a harmonious juxtaposition, mirroring the fusion of my past and present. It's more than just a bakery; it's a manifestation of my growth, a tangible representation of the lessons I've absorbed along the way. This space is a testament to my evolution, a physical embodiment of the values and aspirations that now define me. With each careful detail, I've poured my heart and soul into crafting a haven that feels truly, authentically mine.

"Looks like it's coming together," Greg's voice pulls me from my thoughts, and I turn to see him leaning against the doorway, a smile on his face.

"Yeah," I say, my heart swelling with happiness as he walks over to join me. "It's really happening."

He slips his arm around my waist, pulling me close, and I melt into his embrace, relishing the familiar comfort. I rest my head on his shoulder, taking in the warmth of his presence and the subtle scent of his cologne. The gentle rise and fall of his chest against me is soothing, and grounding. "It's going to be amazing, Sophie. I can already see it," Greg murmurs, his voice a low rumble that I feel as much as hear. His words are filled with genuine excitement and pride, mirroring my own emotions. As we stand there, surveying the room together, I can feel the potential of the space unfurling before us, brimming with possibility.

"I just want it to be a place where people feel at home," I say softly, my gaze sweeping over the space. "Where they can come in, relax, and enjoy a little piece of Buttercup Bay."

Greg kisses my forehead, his lips warm against my skin. "You've created something special here. And you're right—you've made this place feel like home, just like you've made this town feel like home for me. I'm glad that you wanted to rent the place next door and add on to Buttercup Bakes."

His words wrap around my heart, filling me with a sense of belonging that I never expected in a small town like this. The warmth of his embrace and the sincerity in his voice make me feel truly at home. "I never thought I'd end up here," I admit, my voice tinged with wonder and a hint of disbelief. "But now that I'm here, I can't imagine being anywhere else." I pause, taking in the cozy atmosphere we've created together. "It's funny how life leads you to exactly where you're meant to be, even when you least expect it."

He smiles, turning me to face him. "It's funny how life works out, isn't it? We both found something we didn't even know we were looking for."

I nod, my heart full as I look into his eyes, seeing the future we're building together reflected back at me. "And we're just getting started."

As we stand there, basking in the warmth of our shared moment, the front door suddenly swings open with a creak. Mrs. Whittaker bustles in, her cheeks flushed from the crisp outdoor air. She's closely followed by Emma, laden with bulging bags of supplies, the handles straining against the weight. The two of them bring a flurry of activity into our quiet space, their entrance a stark contrast to the intimate atmosphere we'd created just moments before.

"We brought you a few things to help you get started," Mrs. Whittaker says, her tone brisk but kind. "Thought you might need them."

Emma grins, setting down her bag on one of the countertops. "You didn't think we'd let you open this place without a little help from your family, did you?"

I laugh, my heart swelling with gratitude as I realize how much I've come to rely on these people—these friends who have welcomed me into their community with open arms. "Thank you. Really, I couldn't have done any of this without you."

Mrs. Whittaker waves off my thanks with a dismissive hand. "Nonsense. You're part of this town now, Sophie. We take care of our own."

Her words bring a lump to my throat, and I blink back the sudden rush of emotion. This town, this place—it's become more than just a stop on my journey. It's become home, in every sense of the word.

As we unpack the supplies, the space starts to come alive, taking on a warmth and character that feels distinctly mine. Greg moves around the room, helping where he can, his presence grounding me in a way that nothing else ever has. This is our future, the life we're building together, and I couldn't be more excited.

"Have you thought about what you'll do for the grand opening?" Emma asks, pulling me from my thoughts.

I smile, a plan already forming in my mind. "I was thinking of doing a mix of my favorite city-inspired pastries and some classic Buttercup Bay recipes. Something that shows where I've come from and where I am now. Combined with some of the favorites from Greg's, of course."

Greg nods, his eyes lighting up. "That sounds perfect. A little bit of both worlds, just like you."

We spend the rest of the afternoon planning the grand opening, tossing around ideas, and making lists of everything we need to do. The townspeople stop by throughout the day, offering their help, their advice, and their encouragement. It's overwhelming in the best possible way, a reminder of just how much I've come to belong here.

Later, after everyone has left, Greg and I sit together in the dim light of the bakery, the plans for our future spread out on the table before us. We talk about the bakery, about the possibilities of expanding our business together, about the life we're building here. And for the first time, we even talk about the idea of starting a family someday—a thought that fills me with excitement and a deep, settled peace.

"This is where I want to be," I say softly, my hand resting on top of his. "With you, building this life together."

Greg squeezes my hand, his eyes filled with love. "And I wouldn't want to be anywhere else. We've got a future here, Sophie—a future I'm so excited to share with you."

As I look around the bakery, at the space we're creating, at the plans we're making, I feel a deep sense of contentment settle over me. This is where I belong, with the man I love, in a town that has become my home.

And as we close the door behind us, stepping out into the cool evening air, I know that the life I've always wanted is right here, in Buttercup Bay, with Greg by my side.

CHAPTER 14

Greg

THE MORNING SUN filters through the windows of Sophie's side of the bakery, casting a warm glow over the sleek countertops and vintage décor that fill the space. The grand opening is just getting started, and already the room is buzzing with the sound of laughter and excited chatter. The scent of freshly baked pastries wafts through the air, mingling with the rich aroma of brewed coffee. It's the kind of morning that makes you feel alive, and as I stand behind the counter, watching Sophie greet each customer with a smile, I can't help but feel a deep sense of pride and contentment.

Sophie's done it. She's created something truly special here—a place that perfectly blends her city sophistication with the warmth and charm of Buttercup Bay. The bakery is a reflection of her journey, a symbol of the life we're building together. And as I look around at the crowd that's gathered to celebrate, I feel the full embrace of this town's love and acceptance, not just for Sophie, but for both of us.

"Greg, you've got to try these," Emma calls from across the room, waving a plate of pastries in my direction. "Sophie's outdone herself."

I grin, making my way over to her and taking a bite of one of the delicate pastries. It's as delicious as it looks, and I can't help but feel a surge of pride for Sophie. "She sure has," I agree, savoring the sweet, buttery flavor. "She's put her heart into this place."

Emma nods, her eyes twinkling with approval. "You both have. This bakery—it's the perfect blend of everything you've brought to this town. And I think everyone here feels that."

I glance around the room, taking in the sight of friends, neighbors, and even a few out-of-towners, all enjoying the space we've created. There's a sense of community here, a feeling of belonging that's almost tangible. And as I watch Sophie move through the crowd, laughing and chatting with everyone, I realize just how much this town has come to mean to both of us.

For so long, I worried that I wasn't enough, that I'd have to prove myself to keep Sophie by my side. But seeing her here, surrounded by the people who have welcomed her with open arms, I know that I never had to prove anything. She loves me for who I am, just as this town has always accepted me. And now, she's found her place here too.

The celebration is in full swing, the air electric with joy and laughter, when Sophie finally makes her way over to me, weaving through the crowd with a radiant smile. Her eyes are shining with unbridled happiness, reflecting the twinkling lights strung up around us. She reaches for my hand, giving it a gentle squeeze as she leans in close.

"Can you believe it?" she says, her voice filled with excitement and wonder. Her cheeks are flushed from the festivities, and I can feel the warmth of her enthusiasm. "I never imagined it would turn out like this. It's like a dream come true, isn't it? Everyone here, celebrating together... it's more than I ever dared to hope for."

I smile, wrapping my arm around her waist and pulling her close. "You've done an incredible job, Sophie. This place is everything you dreamed it would be—and more."

She leans into me, her head resting on my shoulder as we watch the festivities unfold. "I couldn't have done it without you, Greg. You've been my rock through all of this."

"And you've been mine," I reply, pressing a kiss to the top of her head. "We make a pretty good team, don't we?"

She looks up at me, her eyes filled with love. "The best."

For a moment, we stand there in silence, just soaking in the atmosphere. The bakery is alive with the sound of clinking cups, the hum of conversation, and the occasional burst of laughter. It's everything I hoped it would be. And as I hold Sophie close, I can't help but feel that we're exactly where we're meant to be.

"Come on," I say, gently guiding her toward a quiet corner of the bakery. "Let's take a moment for ourselves."

We slip away from the crowd, finding a small table by the window where we can watch the town square outside. The sun is shining, the leaves are beginning to turn, and everything feels just right.

Sophie takes my hand, her fingers warm against mine. "This is it, isn't it? The life we've been working toward."

I nod, feeling a deep sense of satisfaction settle over me. "It is. And it's just the beginning."

She smiles, her eyes glimmering with a mix of happiness and anticipation. "I can't wait to see what the future holds for us."

"Neither can I," I say, squeezing her hand. "We've talked about expanding the bakery, maybe even integrating our businesses more closely. And who knows? Maybe one day, we'll have a little one running around here too."

Her smile widens at the thought, and I can see the excitement in her eyes. "I'd love that, Greg. I really would."

There's a warmth in her voice, a certainty that tells me she's ready for whatever comes next. And as I look into her eyes, I know that I am too. We've built something beautiful here—something that's grounded in love, trust, and a deep sense of belonging. And I can't wait to see where our journey takes us next.

As the afternoon wears on, the celebration continues, with friends and neighbors stopping by to offer their congratulations and support. The bakery is filled with laughter, warmth, and the unmistakable feeling of community. And as I stand by Sophie's side, greeting each guest with a smile, I know that we're not just building a business here—we're building a life.

By the time the sun begins to set, the bakery is still buzzing with energy, but there's a quiet contentment that's settled over the room. Sophie and I step outside, hand in hand, to watch the last rays of sunlight dip below the horizon. The town square is bathed in a golden glow, and everything feels right in the world.

As we stand there, I pull her close, my heart full to bursting. "We did it, Sophie. We've built something amazing here."

She looks up at me, her eyes shining with tears of happiness. "We did. And I couldn't have done it without you."

I smile, leaning down to kiss her, my lips brushing softly against hers. It's a kiss filled with love, with gratitude, and with the promise of everything that's still to come. When we finally pull back, we're both breathless, but there's a sense of peace that lingers between us. The warmth of her body against mine feels like home, and I can't help but marvel at how far we've come. The fading light catches in her hair, turning it to spun gold, and I'm struck once again by how beautiful she is, inside and out. In this moment, surrounded by the fruits of our labor and the love we've nurtured, I know that whatever challenges lie ahead, we'll face them together, just as we always have.

"We belong here, don't we?" she whispers, her voice filled with wonder.

"We do," I reply, my voice steady and sure. "And we always will."

As we stand there, the town square quieting down as the day comes to an end, I know that we've found our place in this world. Buttercup Bay has become our home, and with Sophie by my side, I know that we're exactly where we're meant to be.

The future stretches out before us, bright and full of possibility. And as we walk back inside, hand in hand, I can't wait to see what it holds for us.

CHAPTER 15

Sophie

THE HALLOWEEN BASH is in full swing, the town square glowing with a warm, festive light that seems to wrap Buttercup Bay in a blanket of comfort and joy. Pumpkins of all shapes and sizes line the streets, their carved faces flickering with the soft glow of candles. The scent of cinnamon, apples, and bonfires fills the air, mingling with the sound of laughter and music. It's a night of celebration, a night that marks not only the passing of another year but the anniversary of when everything changed for me.

Children dart between costumed adults, their excited squeals punctuating the crisp autumn air. Strings of twinkling orange and purple lights crisscross overhead, casting a magical glow on the revelers below. The old oak tree in the center of the square stands as a silent sentinel, its branches adorned with paper lanterns swaying gently in the breeze. Booths line the perimeter, offering everything from caramel apples to fortune telling, their cheerful attendants calling out to passersby. As I stand there, taking it all in, I can't help but marvel at how much has happened in just one year and how this festive night now holds a deeper meaning for me than I ever could have imagined.

Greg's hand is warm in mine as we walk through the square, the crowd parting to greet us with smiles and waves. It's hard to believe that just a year ago, I was standing in this very spot, unsure of where I belonged, uncertain about the life I wanted to live. But now, as I look around at the faces of friends, neighbors, and loved ones, I know without a doubt that I've found my place.

"Can you believe it's been a year already?" Greg asks, his voice low and filled with the same sense of wonder that's been with us all day.

I smile up at him, squeezing his hand. "It feels like we've been here forever, doesn't it? But at the same time, it feels like it's gone by so fast."

He nods, his gaze soft as he looks at me. "Time flies when you're building the life you've always wanted."

We stop for a moment, taking it all in—the joy on the faces of the children as they run from booth to booth, the contentment of the older couples sitting on benches, sipping hot cider, and the sense of belonging that fills the air. This town, this community, has become so much more than just a place to live. It's become home in every sense of the word.

Buttercup Bakes stands proudly at the heart of the square, its windows glowing with a warm, inviting light that spills out onto the cobblestone street. It's bustling with activity, even on a crisp autumn night like this, as people pop in for a quick treat or just to say hello to familiar faces. The chalkboard menu propped outside is filled with seasonal specials—pumpkin spice everything, of course, along with cinnamon apple pies and maple pecan tarts—and the rustic charm of the space has only deepened over the past year.

Every corner of the bakery tells a story, from the antique rolling pin display to the well-worn wooden countertops. It's a story of where I've come from, the challenges I've faced, and where I'm going, a testament to the dreams I've poured into this little slice of heaven. The aroma of freshly baked bread and sweet pastries wafts through the air, drawing in passersby and regulars alike, each one becoming a part of the bakery's ever-growing tale.

"I think the bakery has become everyone's favorite spot," Greg says, following my gaze. "They can't seem to get enough of it."

I laugh softly. "And I can't seem to get enough of them. This town... it's everything I didn't know I needed."

Greg pulls me closer, pressing a kiss to my temple. "And you're everything I didn't know I needed, Sophie. This past year has been the best of my life, and it's all because of you."

His words warm me from the inside out, filling me with a sense of love and gratitude that's almost overwhelming. "I feel the same way, Greg. I never imagined that I'd find a place where I feel so completely at home or someone who makes me feel so loved."

He turns me to face him, his eyes filled with the same love that's been there since the day we first met. "You've brought so much light into my life, Sophie. And I can't wait to see what the future holds for us."

As we stand there, wrapped in each other's arms, I can't help but think about the future—the plans we've made, the dreams we're still dreaming. The bakery has become a symbol of everything we've built together. As we talk about expanding our businesses, and integrating our lives even more, I know that we're just getting started.

The sound of laughter draws our attention, and I see Emma standing nearby, watching us with a smile tinged with a hint of wistfulness. She's been a constant presence in our lives, Greg's sister, who has become like family to me, and I know she's happy for us. But I also know that she's still searching for her own place in the world, her own happily ever after.

"Emma," I call out, waving her over. "Come join us."

She walks over, her smile widening as she takes in the sight of us. "You two are just too perfect, you know that?"

I laugh, shaking my head. "Hardly perfect, but we're happy. And that's what matters."

Emma nods, her gaze softening as she looks at the bakery. "You've built something amazing here, Sophie. And you've made this town even more special just by being a part of it."

Her words bring a lump to my throat, and I blink back the tears that threaten to spill over. "Thank you, Emma. That means more to me than you know."

She smiles, a touch of wistfulness in her expression. "I'm happy for you, Sophie. You deserve all of this."

As we stand there, talking and laughing, I can't help but wonder what the future holds for Emma. She's strong, independent, and full of life, and I have no doubt that she'll find her own path, her own place where she belongs. And maybe, just maybe, she'll find the love she's been waiting for.

The night deepens, the festivities continuing around us, and as Greg and I walk hand in hand through the square, surrounded by the people who have become our family, I feel a sense of peace settle over me. This is where I belong—here, in this town, with Greg by my side, surrounded by a community that has embraced me with open arms.

As we make our way back to the bakery, the warm glow of the lights guiding us home, I can't help but feel a deep sense of gratitude. I've found everything I was searching for—and so much more. I'm loved, accepted, and fulfilled, and for the first time in my life, I feel truly at home.

The future is bright, and full of possibilities, and I know that whatever comes next, we'll face it together. Greg and I have built something beautiful here, and as we continue to dream and plan, I know that the best is yet to come.

As we step inside the bakery, the warmth of the space enveloping us, I glance at Greg, my heart swelling with love. "Ready to see what the next year brings?"

He smiles, pulling me close. "With you by my side? Absolutely."

And as we close the door behind us, I know that our journey is just beginning. Buttercup Bay is more than just a town—it's our home, our future, and the place where we've found everything we were looking for.

And as I look ahead, I can't wait to see where the road takes us next.

If you enjoyed this book, take a moment to leave a review. This allows your fellow readers to determine if this is a good book for them.

Thank you!